Ada Lace,

Take Me to Your Leader

ALSO BY EMILY CALANDRELLI

Ada Lace, on the Case
Ada Lace Sees Red

Ada Lace,

Take Me to Your Leader

• AN ADA LACE ADVENTURE •

EMILY CALANDRELLI

WITH TAMSON WESTON

ILLUSTRATED BY RENÉE KURILLA

Simon & Schuster Books for Young Readers

New York London Toronto Sydney New Delhi

For the kid who daydreams about aliens.
You're the normal one.
—E. C.

For Evan
—T. W.

For all the ISS crew members who take time to communicate with students of the world. I think you're pretty awesome!
—R. K.

SIMON & SCHUSTER BOOKS FOR YOUNG READERS
An imprint of Simon & Schuster Children's Publishing Division
1230 Avenue of the Americas, New York, New York 10020

For information about special discounts for bulk purchases, please contact Simon & Schuster Special Sales at 1-866-506-1949 or business@simonandschuster.com.
The Simon & Schuster Speakers Bureau can bring authors to your live event. For more information or to book an event, contact the Simon & Schuster Speakers Bureau at 1-866-248-3049 or visit our website at www.simonspeakers.com.
Also available in a Simon & Schuster Books for Young Readers hardcover edition
Book design by Laurent Linn
The text for this book was set in Minister Std.
The illustrations for this book were rendered digitally.
Manufactured in the United States of America | 0318 OFF
First Simon & Schuster Books for Young Readers paperback edition May 2018
2 4 6 8 10 9 7 5 3 1
Library of Congress Cataloging-in-Publication Data
Names: Calandrelli, Emily, author. | Weston, Tamson, author. | Illustrator. Kurilla, Renée,
Title: Ada Lace, take me to your leader / Emily Calandrelli ; with Tamson Weston ; illustrated by Renée Kurilla.
Description: First edition. | New York : Simon & Schuster Books for Young Readers, [2018] | Series: An Ada Lace adventure ; [3] | Summary: When eight-year-old Ada uses her love of science and technology to tinker with a ham radio, Nina hears sounds that she thinks are space aliens.
Identifiers: LCCN 2017018866| ISBN 9781481486057 (hardcover) | ISBN 9781481486040 (pbk.) | ISBN 9781481486064 (eBook)
Subjects: | CYAC: Mystery and detective stories. | Amateur radio stations—Fiction. | Astronauts—Fiction. | Science—Methodology—Fiction. | Friendship—Fiction.
Classification: LCC PZ7.1.C28 Ah 2018 | DDC [Fic]—dc23
LC record available at https://lccn.loc.gov/2017018866

Ada Lace,

Take Me to Your Leader

Chapter One

Radio Silence

Ada pressed the button on the mic and opened her mouth to speak. That was the exact moment when Ms. Lace burned the toast. The smoke alarm on the stairs went off, and George the robot rolled around the room crying, "Fire! Fire!"

"NO!" Ada yelled. "George, there is no fire!"

Then the sprinkler in the center of Ada's bedroom ceiling rained down on her bed, her rug, and her desk. Ada threw her raincoat over the radio, but she wasn't sure she was quick enough.

"George, the fire's out!" called Ada.

"Emergency averted," answered George. The fire alarm stopped beeping, the sprinkler stopped sprinkling. Elliott ran into Ada's room with his new Batman umbrella.

"Aw, I missed it again."

"Ada," said Mr. Lace from the doorway, "you may need to fine-tune George."

"Mom may need to fine-tune the toaster."

"Ada . . . ," said Mr. Lace.

"I know, Dad. I'll fix him." Ada had engineered her robot, George, to keep her room safe, but she had already had to replace her rug after their neighbor Jacob grilled his steak in the courtyard and the smoke poured into Ada's room. Clearly, George was doing his job a little too well.

"Safety first," said George. It was as if he'd read her thoughts.

"That's creepy, George," said Ada.

The night-light on George's head lit up. "This will comfort you," he said. Soothing music drifted out of his speakers.

"Thanks, George, I feel better now. You can go to sleep," said Ada. He rolled into the corner and turned off.

Ada pulled the raincoat off her ham radio and dried it off. Then Nina showed up. Ada looked at the clock and realized she was supposed to meet her friend five minutes ago to walk to school.

"Hey, you were late, so I thought I would just run over here. Whoa! Is that a ham radio?"

"Yes! Mr. Peebles gave it to me the other day. I'm still trying to figure it out. How did you know?"

"I was just reading about them in my book *World of Weird Book 3: Across the Void*! Have you contacted a parallel universe yet?"

"I'm not sure I can even talk to Mr. Peebles now. George may have broken it."

"George used it?"

"It's a long story. I can tell you on the way to school."

• • •

As they walked, Ada told Nina about George's false alarm, and Nina told Ada about her book. In it a group of kids used a ham radio in their clubhouse. First, they talked to people all over the world, then, from . . . other worlds.

"That sounds cool," said Ada. "I wish I could do that with my radio."

"Maybe you can!" said Nina.

"At this point I'd be happy just to talk to someone in Oakland."

After school, Ada invited Nina over to help her work on the radio. Nina had all kinds of advice.

"You know, in the book Nate and Fiona wore tinfoil hats."

"Oh. Really? Why?"

"Gee, Ada, I thought you knew about this

stuff. That way the evil energy from the other world couldn't seep into their brains."

"I think I'll just start with trying to figure out how to talk to someone in the Bay Area first. Baby steps. Anyway, you need a different kind of radio to speak to other parts of the world. And, uh, probably *other* worlds, I guess."

"Why is it called a ham radio anyway?" asked Nina.

Ada's dad was passing Ada's room. He couldn't resist a chance to answer. "Well, rumor has it that Marconi was a little hungry when he invented radio. So, the first thing he did when he got it working was order a ham sandwich!"

"Dad!" called Ada.

"Is that true?" asked Nina.

"Of course not!" said Ada.

"Yeah, you're right. Marconi was Italian.

He probably would have ordered capicola or prosciutto."

"Ugh!" said Ada.

Nina didn't seem to know whether to be amused or confused.

"No one really knows why it's called a ham," said Ada. "Some people think it's an acronym for the three radio innovators: Hertz, Armstrong, and Marconi, but there are other explanations too."

Ada took the cover off the radio and revealed a bunch of brightly colored wires and little nodes fixed to a green circuit board.

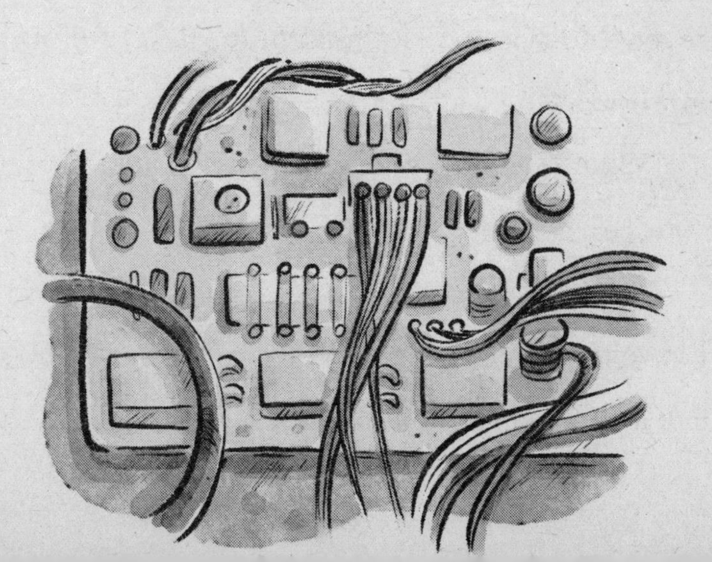

"Gosh! It's so pretty. The cover should be see-through!" said Nina.

"That's a cool idea. Maybe I'll work on that after I figure out the talking part."

There was very little moisture inside from the fire emergency. Still, Ada patted the whole thing down with a towel, just in case. Then she put the casing back on, flicked on the switch, and pressed the button on the microphone.

Kilo Delta Eight Papa Kilo Romeo. Anyone out there? Over.

KD8PKR looking for someone to talk to. Anyone? Mr. Peebles?

"What's KD whatchamacallit? Is it a secret code?"

"It's my call sign. I got it with my radio license. I have to use it whenever I talk on ham radio. It's like a . . . special radio name."

The radio answered with static. Ada grabbed an antenna she had saved from her dad's old transistor radio. It was longer than the antenna on the ham, so she swapped them. Still, all she heard was static.

"I don't understand why it's not working."

"Can we add something to it? Like a paper clip?"

"I don't know about a paper clip . . . but I

think I saw somewhere that people use aluminum foil."

"I'll go get it!" said Nina.

Nina ran down to the kitchen and grabbed a roll of aluminum foil. She brought it back upstairs. They ripped a piece off and attached it to the antenna.

After a few hours of tinkering, it was time for dinner.

"I can't believe the signal is still so weak," said Ada. "Maybe the buildings are blocking it."

"Maybe we should try a Ouija board," said Nina.

"Like I said, I think we have to start with somewhere in our own realm first," said Ada. "Anyway, I don't have a Ouija board. I think the antenna needs to be higher up."

"Like on the roof!" said Nina.

"Exactly."

Ada asked for Mr. Lace's help. Her parents had set some pretty firm rules about Ada climbing things after she'd broken her ankle over the summer. Mr. Lace went through the attic window and attached Ada's ham antenna to the roof, just above Ada's window. Even with the extra height, though, Ada and Nina heard mostly static.

• • •

Ada and Nina tried for the rest of the night to contact someone but they had no luck.

"Bedtime! Bedtime!" said George.

"It's not a school night, George," said Ada. "I can go to bed a little later tonight."

"Ada!" called Ms. Lace. "It's time for bed."

Ada looked at the clock. It was ten.

"Wow," said Ada. "You were right, George."

Ada was about to turn off the radio, then stopped.

"Maybe we should keep it on. You know, in case it starts working," said Ada.

"You know, you're right. It could be morning for them in the middle of the night," said Nina.

"For whom?" asked Ada.

"The beings from the other world!"

Chapter Two

Strange Encounters

Nina woke Ada in the middle of the night. She was frantic.

"Ada! They're trying to talk to us!" she whispered loudly.

"What? Who?"

"I don't know. But someone. Or *something*!"

George woke up too. The little light Ada had installed on the top of his head glowed.

"Everything will be all right," said George. He started playing "Three Little Birds" by Bob Marley. It was a song that Ada's mom used to sing to her when she was very small.

"See," said Ada. "Listen to George. He knows what he's talking about."

"You don't understand! I heard something. It sounded . . . alien. Like high-pitched beeps and pops. Probably alien speech."

"There are some funny noises on hams, I think. You were probably still dreaming, and that made it sound extra strange. George, play Nina a lullaby," said Ada.

A simple version of Brahms's "Lullaby" played over George's speakers.

"Does that make you feel better?" asked Ada.

"No. It was not a dream," said Nina. "I know what a dream is like."

"Okay. But remember Occam's razor?" asked Ada. "The right answer—"

"—is usually the simplest one," said Nina. "I guess . . ."

"Well, whatever you heard, the radio is quiet now," said Ada. "I almost wish you *did* hear something—"

"No, you don't," said Nina. She sounded really spooked. Ada had never seen her like that before. She usually seemed pretty excited by her kooky ideas.

"Okay," said Ada, getting out of bed. "Let's see if we can contact anyone."

Ada walked over to the radio and turned up the volume a bit. There was just the hissing of static. She pressed the button for the mic.

Kilo Delta Eight Papa Kilo Romeo. Anyone up for a chat?

No one responded.

This is KD8PKR. Hello? Is someone up?

Ada spoke a few more times but didn't reach anyone. She searched through different frequencies but heard no weird sounds.

"I'm sorry I woke you up," said Nina.

"It's okay," said Ada. "That book has probably gotten into your head."

Ada woke the next morning to find her friend already awake. Nina had her back pressed against the far wall. She had wrapped herself in her sleeping bag and was staring suspiciously at the radio across the room.

"Nina? What's up?" Ada asked. "Are the creatures from beyond calling again?"

"They said . . ." Nina paused. She swallowed. "They said, 'Release the swarm!' They're coming for us, Ada."

"Oh, Nina. I think you need some sleep."

"I heard it!" cried Nina. "It was faint, but I know what I heard."

Ada went to the radio. She realized she had left it on scan. She tried again to call other operators and heard a few faint, ghostly voices, but it was mostly just static.

"Nina," said Ada.

"I'm not crazy, Ada!"

"I know you're not," said Ada. But she was beginning to worry about her friend.

• • •

That morning, Mr. Lace made his famous pancakes. Nina barely touched them. In fact, she nearly fell asleep at the table.

"You girls weren't up talking on the radio all night, were you?" asked Ms. Lace. "You look a little sleepy, Nina."

"Nina had some bad dreams," said Ada.

"Let's *hope* they were just dreams," said Nina. Then she went home to take a nap.

Ada went back up to her room to try to get the radio working. After trying a bunch of different positions for the antenna, she gave up. Perhaps Mr. Peebles would know what to do. She headed over to his stoop to find out. He was throwing a ball for his little dog, Alan.

"I've checked all the wiring, extended the antenna, and even moved it to the rooftop to get a better signal," Ada told Mr. Peebles. "But I just can't connect with anyone. George set the sprinkler off yesterday morning. Do you think that did it?"

"Was the radio open when it happened? Did the wires or any of the connections get wet?"

"No. I threw my raincoat over it pretty quickly, and I made sure to wipe it down afterward, but there wasn't much to wipe off."

"Huh," said Mr. Peebles. "Well you said you heard some things. What kinds of things are you hearing?"

"Faint voices, mostly. Nina thinks she heard something," said Ada, "But it's a little far-fetched."

"What did she hear?" asked Mr. Peebles.

"She thinks she heard aliens," said Ada. Ada noticed Milton Edison lurking by the fountain with his remote control car. Milton didn't seem to be listening, but who knew with him? He couldn't be trusted.

"You know Milton has a ham radio," Mr. Peebles said. He must have seen her noticing Milton. "Perhaps you two could try to communicate with each other."

"Uh, yeah, maybe." *Not a chance*, Ada thought to herself. Milton was a sneak and a cheater. Why did he have to do everything that she did?

"So, what do you think I should do, Mr. Peebles?" Ada asked.

"It's been a while since I used my old Heathkit

ham," he said, "but the city is pretty hilly. Maybe the signal is being blocked by some high terrain. We may just need to boost it a bit. I have some ideas. Let me do a little research and grab some equipment. Meet me back here in an hour, and we can work on it together."

"Okay," said Ada. She was afraid to get her hopes up. She wasn't asking for much. She just wanted to be able to use her new license and talk to a few people in the area. Why was that so hard?

Chapter Three
The World of Hams

In an hour, Mr. Peebles returned with a black plastic briefcase.

"What's that?" asked Ada. "It doesn't have anything to do with aliens, does it? Because I had my fill of those last night."

"No aliens. I promise," said Mr. Peebles. "This, my young friend, is a radio repeater. I can get a good signal out my back window, but I'd have to have one of these hoisted in a tree out back in order to communicate with people outside our little neighborhood."

"What's it do?"

"This little contraption will take your signal and retransmit it so that you can connect with people over a broader area. You see, your signal is probably having trouble making it over these high trees we have in Juniper Garden."

"Wow. What's in there?"

Mr. Peebles opened the box. He showed Ada two handheld radios connected by wires to a little white box with a switch on it.

"This radio receives the signal," said Mr. Peebles, pointing to one radio. "It transmits it to this little white box. The white box then relays it to this radio over here." He tapped the second radio. "The signal comes out of the transmitting radio twice as strong!"

"In theory," said Ada. She still didn't want to get her hopes up.

"Well, shall we give it a try?" asked Mr. Peebles.

"Absolutely," said Ada.

Ada got permission from her father to put the repeater in a tall tree not too far from Ada's window. Now the trees that were blocking the signal would actually help her get a better one. Mr. Lace went through the window and tossed the rope over a high branch and looped it around once. Then Mr. Peebles and Ada hoisted the repeater up into the tree using the rope. Then they tied the end of the rope to a lower branch to secure it. Once the repeater was set up, Ada went to her room, and Mr. Peebles went back to his lab to fire up his old Heathkit ham.

This is Kilo Delta Eight Papa Kilo Romeo. Mr. Peebles, are you there? Over.

Kilo Delta Eight Papa Kilo Romeo, this is Kilo Zulu Six Delta. Ada, I can hear you loud and clear. Over.

Great! Nice weather we're having. Over.

The bay area's finest fog. Nothing beats it. Now you can try connecting to other "hams," Ada. Over.

• • •

The repeater worked like a charm! Now she could hear all kinds of people having all kinds of conversations. Even with all the electronics she had, even with her very own security robot, Ada couldn't help being amazed by her radio. People had been using this technology to talk over land and sea for more than a hundred years. And there were no wires involved! Just radio waves. *This is as close to magic as a person gets,* Ada thought. Nina just had to love it like she did. She just had to get her friend to see how amazing her new machine was.

In the meantime, though, Ada had to move past listening to talking. At first Ada felt shy about starting conversations, but the people she heard seemed so nice. After all, what else was a radio for, but to communicate?

First, she talked to a boy from Oakland who

had all kinds of questions about George and how to make his own robot.

Then she spoke to a girl from Marin who was trying to start an engineering club and wanted to know if Ada would join.

She had just connected with a rocket scientist in Alameda, when Mr. Lace popped in.

"You got your radio working!" he said.

"Well. It was mostly Mr. Peebles," said Ada.

"Who are you talking to?"

Ada told her dad about the boy in Oakland and the girl in Marin.

"Now I'm talking to a rocket scientist! She's about to launch a weather balloon!"

"Amazing!"

Mr. Lace listened in with Ada for a little bit and then went back to his office to finish up his lesson plan.

After Mr. Lace left, Ada connected with someone else in her neighborhood who had just gotten his own license.

KD8PKR. This is KD86E. It's a beautiful foggy day here in the Bay Area. Over.

It is indeed! Perfect kite-flying weather, eh? Over.

If only! I just got a new kite! I was going to attach my GoPro to it today.

They talked about kites and cameras for a while. Ada knew he must be really close from the strength of the signal. She was going to see if he wanted to get together the next windy day in Juniper Garden, or maybe Golden Gate Park, but he signed off before she could get his name.

Ada knew this was just the beginning. Today she'd just talked with people in her area, but with an upgrade in equipment and a more advanced license, she could talk to people from all over the world. In the meantime, she suddenly felt like she had a whole new community.

The next day after begging and pleading, and agreeing to go see the newest Wizard Warriors movie with her, Ada convinced Nina to come over and try the radio again. It was clear Nina was still nervous. But Ada thought since her friend was better rested, she might be able to see the radio through fresh eyes and really appreciate the world it opened up. She was excited to show Nina how well the radio was working. She thought for sure that now she would understand how silly her fears were.

"Mr. Peebles knew just how to fix my radio, of course," said Ada. "So now I can talk to people from all over the Bay Area."

"But just *people* people, right?" said Nina, looking wary. "Not green bug people or clouds of pure energy. I mean, you haven't heard from . . . whatever called the other night?"

"They all sounded pretty normal," said Ada. "What you heard must have been a fluke. Or it could have just been a dream. Sometimes when I wake up in the middle of the night, I hear weird things too." She didn't mention that she never thought she heard aliens.

"But it didn't *seem* like a dream. I was dreaming about something completely different before I woke up."

"Well, even still. There's probably a good explanation," said Ada, switching on the power to her repeater. "And I haven't heard anything weird since, so I think we're safe."

Ada and Nina settled down at Ada's desk. Nina was given the seat of honor, in front of the mic. Ada flicked the radio on. Then she realized her headphones were missing.

"Ugh! Elliott! Do you have my headphones again?" she yelled.

"Mr. Pickles and I were playing fighter pilot!" he called back.

Ada ran out of the room to fetch the headphones from her brother and his stuffed pig. In the hallway, she heard the thrilling crackle of her ham. Someone was about to say something! Who could it be? But when she got back into the bedroom, Nina did not look so thrilled.

"I gotta go," said Nina. She was clearly freaked out.

"What? But we haven't even tried it out yet!"

"That thing has a whole life of its own, Ada," said Nina. "You think you control it, but you don't. It just said, 'Take me to your leader.' You wanna know who'd say that? I'll tell you who. It's aliens."

Nina ran from the room, down the stairs, across the garden, and home.

Ada listened for an hour to find the "aliens" Nina heard, with no luck. She stopped to do homework and have dinner, then hopped on the ham again before bed. She heard about a poor man whose car battery died on the side of the 480. His phone was also dead. Thankfully, he had a ham radio and so did his mechanic.

Then she heard a bunch of bird-watchers

talking about what they had spotted in Golden Gate Park that morning. They saw a western tanager, two Allen's hummingbirds and a Nuttall's woodpecker.

Then she heard about a rare humpback whale sighting in San Francisco Bay.

Nina was so worried about creatures from other worlds, that she was missing all of these voices sharing exciting and interesting moments in their lives. The weather had been clear and windy—good for sailing and soccer games—and also good for kite flying. She was eager to reach KD86E—the boy with the kite she'd talked to before. She wondered if he'd had any luck today.

KD86E, are you there? Over.

KD86E, this is KD8PKR. How are you making out with that kite? Over.

KD8PKR. This is KD86E. The kite flying was

EPIC. So good. And I got the GoPro on there too. Picture's a little shaky though. Did you get out today? Over.

Nah. I was trying to reassure my friend that aliens weren't invading Earth. It didn't work. I don't know. Something she heard really freaked her out. Hey, what's your name, anyway? Over.

Ha! Uh . . . my mom says I'm not supposed to say. Sorry! Gotta run. Dinner. Over and out.

Ada looked at the clock. It was nine o'clock. Who ate dinner at nine o'clock on a school night?

"Time for bed. Time for bed," said George. He rolled around in front of Ada's bed, as if showing her where she was supposed to be by now.

"When you're right, you're right, George," said Ada.

Chapter Four

The Alien Resurfaces

On the way to school the next day, Ada couldn't stop talking about the people she had spoken to on the ham radio. She wanted Nina to be excited about it too. She told her about the strange kid who wouldn't tell her his name. And she told her about how she'd heard someone talking about a storm coming off the coast of Catalina. All Nina said was "Mmmm-hmmmm," which was not a Nina response at all. So Ada told her about her plans to get a high-frequency radio, because that would allow her to hear things on the other side of the world.

"Nina, wouldn't it be cool to talk to someone from Sri Lanka? Or South Africa?"

"That does sound cool, Ada. But I always

thought talking to aliens might be cool too. Now that it's happened, I'm not so sure."

"But we still don't know—"

"They said, 'Take me to your leader,' Ada! That's what aliens say. They could be invading right now!"

"Yeah, but that's exactly why it doesn't seem right. I mean, it's a little too perfect, isn't it?" said Ada. "Besides, we don't even know if alien life exists. And if it does, it's probably not going to speak English. It seems like someone was just goofing around."

"They could have translators!" said Nina.

"Are you sure it wasn't George?"

"Does George ever say, 'Release the swarm'?"

"I don't think so, but he surprises me all the time," said Ada.

"Well, it didn't sound like him," said Nina. "And I don't think his little night-light was on."

"Nina. I don't want you missing out on all the fun. I'm sure we'll find out what's going on. Can we try one more time? This afternoon, maybe?"

Nina sighed. "I guess so. I'll come over after school. I just have to stop home first."

Ada was having fun with her radio, but she really wanted to share it. It made her sad that Nina had started out so excited and then gotten so . . . freaked out. She'd always had a vivid imagination, but she'd never scared herself with it!

All day at school the ham radio was in the back of Ada's mind. She really had to make it fun for Nina this time, or she might not ever get her near the radio—or her room—again.

After school, while Nina went home to drop off her things, Ada went upstairs and turned the radio on. George rolled out right away.

"It's time for homework, Ada," said George.

Ada had had fun programming George, but she was regretting some of his functions. He was beginning to sound like her third parent.

"No homework today, George."

"Would you like to play tick-tack-toe?"

"No thanks, George."

She almost felt a little bad for him.

"Time for my nap," said George. He rolled into his corner and shut down.

Ada attached her new microphone to her radio. Mr. Peebles had given it to her. He'd salvaged it from a radio station that was upgrading its equipment. It had a long bar that she pushed to talk, instead of a button like the one on her old mic. She felt like a real radio operator. After all, that's what she was.

Ada had already started to develop a routine. She liked to start out by just lazily turning the

tuner to see what was happening. There was one guy who was planning a charity event for his motorcycle club. A fisherman rescued a little girl in her sailboat. A woman got advice from a veterinary technician named Betsy on how to safely move a litter of kittens she had found in her garden shed. That's when Nina showed up. She was wearing a tinfoil hat. Ada turned down the volume.

"That looks surprisingly good on you," said Ada. "Trying to keep out the bad energy?"

"Oh, I don't know," said Nina. "It's worth a shot."

"Well, nobody's released any swarms this afternoon that I've heard about," said Ada. "Listen to this—I think it might make you feel better."

How many babies are there, ma'am? Over.

Four . . . five . . . six. I can see six. There might be

more. They're awfully funny looking. Over.

"What kind of babies is she talking about?" Nina asked. She seemed unsure of how to feel about them. Ada got the sense she thought they might be alien spawn.

"Kittens," said Ada.

"Awwww . . ." Who could be suspicious of kittens?

And you said they've been there how long? Over.

About a week now. They're quite small. Over.

Okay. Is the mama kitty still there? Over.

Yes. She was hanging around for a few weeks, and then all of a sudden we didn't see her anymore. Then, surprise! Here she is with her babies. Over.

Do you think she'll let you touch her? Over.

Probably. I've been feeding her for quite a while. Over.

Okay. So you'll want to find a box and put a nice cozy blanket in there. . . .

Nina and Ada listened as Betsy coached the woman through her task. By the end of the conversation the litter had been safely moved to the sunroom in the woman's house.

"That's so cool!" said Nina. She took off her tinfoil hat. "And you talk to people too?"

"Yup. All the time," said Ada. "You wanna try it?"

"Yeah!"

Ada contacted the woman with the weather balloon and let Nina say hi. Then they talked to the kid from Oakland. After a while, they got hungry, so Ada signed off and got up to get some snacks.

"You're not going to leave me alone here with this thing, are you?"

"Nina! We've been having so much fun."

"Yeah, because you were here. But if you leave—"

"I'll tell you what. I'll just bribe Elliott to bring us up a bag of cheesy popcorn."

Ada reached into the jar where she kept all her coolest doodads and pulled out a little Star Fighter figurine to offer Elliott. It was his favorite comic book character. She had no sooner walked through the door than she heard the radio crackle to life behind her. And then she heard the voice.

TAKE ME TO YOUR LEADER! TAKE ME TO YOUR LEADER!

"ADA!" cried Nina.

After a brief pause she heard the voice again.

TAKE ME TO YOUR LEADER.

The signal was as clear as a bell, which meant it was quite close. And Ada recognized the voice. She had been speaking to this person for days, and it had taken this prank for her to realize who it was. Ada looked through the window. Across the garden she saw someone peeking from behind the curtain covering Milton Edison's window.

Chapter Five

Not an Alien. Just a Pest.

Ada thought for a moment about how to handle Milton. He hadn't really broken any rules, but it was just bad radio manners! None of the other hams she had spoken with had tried to trick anyone. They'd all been pretty friendly and helpful. Ada wanted to scare Milton, but not too badly. And she didn't want to break any rules herself. So she would use her call sign clearly and speak forcefully. She put her headphones back on, pressed the bar on the mic, and spoke.

This is KD8PKR. You are breaking the rules agreed upon by the ham community. Please stop or I will be forced to report you. Over.

There was a long pause and then—

TAKE ME TO YOUR LEADER!

Seriously, Milton. Knock it off, or I'll make sure no one in the ham community wants to talk to you again.

Then there was silence—for good, this time. Ada and Nina sat in front of the radio for another ten minutes. Ada spun the dial through all the frequencies used by the ham radio community. Milton didn't turn up again.

"I've been talking to him all week!" said

Ada. "How could I not know it was him?"

"I don't know, Ada," said Nina. "I really don't."

"You didn't know either! You thought he was an alien!" said Ada.

"I wasn't far off!" said Nina.

"I was fooled because he was being so normal. He actually seemed kind of . . . *nice*."

"Wow. That *is* weird. Maybe even weirder than aliens."

"Well, I guess that's taken care of," said Ada. "No aliens. Just the usual suspect."

"I don't know, Ada," said Nina.

"What do you mean? It was clearly Milton."

"He was the daytime alien, but he definitely wasn't the one who said, 'Release the swarm.' That was different. It was more distant sounding . . . and a little creepier. If that was a prank, it was way too clever for Milton to pull off."

Ada gave up trying to convince Nina and let her friend go home. She didn't want to spend any more time on make-believe aliens.

The next three afternoons and evenings Ada spent alone with her ham radio. It seemed like she and Nina hardly saw each other. Ada spent quite a while one afternoon talking to the woman in Alameda with the weather balloon. She was just about to try to call the girl in Marin when she heard from Milton.

KD8PKR? This is KD86E. Are you there? Over.

She almost forgot for a second that he was the same prankster who lived across the courtyard. She almost forgot to be mad at him. She was just about to pick up the mic and talk to him when she remembered.

KD8PKR? Are you there? Over.

Ada ignored it. Why should she talk to Milton Edison when there were so many other more interesting people in the world?

KD8PKR? I'm building this really cool attachment for the GoPro. You wanna see it? Over.

Ada, you're not really still mad, are you? I mean, I didn't do anything wrong, really. It was just a joke! I know we've never really been friends, but I thought we were getting along okay on the radio. Over.

Yeah, because you tricked me! And then you scared the living daylights out of poor Nina! Over.

I didn't think she'd get so scared. I just thought it would be funny. And it was. A little bit. Wasn't it? Over.

It was a little funny. But Ada wasn't going to give Milton Edison the satisfaction of knowing it.

Listen, Milton. I wish you luck with your kite. But I'd rather talk to people who use their radios for good and not evil. Over and out.

Chapter Six

An Exciting World

On Saturday, Ada asked Nina to visit the California Academy of Sciences with her and Mr. Peebles. There was a part of her that really wanted to spend the day on the radio again, but she also missed hanging out with Nina. Nina might never trust the radio, so Ada decided that they should find other things to do together.

Mr. Peebles volunteered at the Cal Academy, and he knew a lot about the building and all the best exhibits. Ada had been there before, and she often wanted to see so much that she could get overwhelmed. Mr. Peebles knew just where to go first.

Nina might have spent the whole afternoon just at the entrance, and Ada couldn't blame her.

There was so much to see before you even walked in. The roof was like a rolling field, covered with grass and plants. There were little round windows all over it that looked like portholes in a ship. Mr. Peebles explained that the roof was called a "living roof." It collected 98 percent of the rainwater. Most buildings allowed the rain to slide off the roof, collecting contaminants that then poured into the local waterways and ecosystem. This roof absorbed the rain and let it nourish plant life. The little portholes were part of a system that helped keep the temperature cool without air conditioners.

The inside of the museum was full of sunlight and activity. Lots of visitors were milling about,

checking their maps and planning their days. Some just stood staring at the beautiful skylit ceiling.

Usually it was hard for Ada to decide where to start. Today they had help from Mr. Peebles. Since the Swamp was near the entrance, they went to see Claude first. Claude was an albino alligator who was rescued from Florida. He was nearly blind, and his skin was white, so he wasn't able to camouflage himself. Claude wouldn't have been able to survive in the wild. The staff used a big red paddle to push fish and pellets toward Claude, so he didn't have to hunt for food.

"Awww . . . I never thought an alligator was cute before—except for Randolph, my stuffed alligator," said Nina.

Ada laughed.

They watched jellyfish in the aquarium drift

around their tank like bright, soft umbrellas.

"Who needs aliens when there are these things?" said Nina.

"You should see the really deep-sea creatures," said Mr. Peebles. "I think they must be the closest thing to alien life on Earth."

"As far as you know," said Nina.

"Speaking of which. Can we go watch the meteor show now?" asked Ada.

"I think we still have about fifteen minutes until it starts. Want to grab a quick peek at the birds and the butterflies first?"

"Yes!" said Nina.

Ada had to admit the third level of the rain forest was pretty spectacular, if a little muggy. It smelled like leaves and rain, and there were more kinds of butterflies and birds than Ada had ever seen. A blue morpho butterfly tried to hitch a ride on Nina on the way out. She named him Frank.

"Nina, you can't take him with you," said Ada.

"I know," Nina said, coaxing the butterfly onto her finger. She placed him on a plant nearby.

"Someday you'll be free, Frank."

"No, he won't, Nina."

"Come on, Ada. Let the poor guy dream," said Nina. "Besides, I have faith in Frank. He looks resourceful."

PLANETARIUM
ENTRANCE

Ada's favorite part of the whole place was the Morrison Planetarium. At the asteroid exhibit, they learned about impact craters, what happens to objects when they hit the atmosphere, and how scientists at the Center for Near Earth Object Studies at NASA planned to prevent large asteroids from hitting the Earth.

There was also an exhibit about Earth and its climate, which was unusual for a planetarium. On the wall was a big quote by a man named Wallace Broecker. It said, "The climate system is an angry beast and we are poking at it with sticks." Mr. Peebles explained that the Morrison Planetarium wanted to treat the Earth like any other planet because, obviously, it was!

"By using groups of small satellites, NASA can study weather patterns, changes in temperature, and pollution levels," said the recorded tour.

• • •

As they rode the streetcar back to Juniper Garden, Ada and Nina talked about Claude, Frank, the jellyfish, asteroids, and the Near Earth Object program at NASA. They had lots of questions about NASA and the tiny satellite program.

"You know, you can listen to NASA on your ham radio, Ada," Mr. Peebles said. "You might even be able to talk to an astronaut."

"No way! Really?" said Ada. "How?"

"I'm surprised I didn't mention it before," said

Mr. Peebles. "The astronauts are often working, so you have to call them during their downtime. Do you want to plan a time to contact them?"

"Yes!" said Ada. "That would be so cool. Wouldn't it, Nina?" If astronauts couldn't lure Nina back to the radio, what could?

"Uh, maybe . . . ," said Nina.

"I'll look into it," said Mr. Peebles.

Ada felt more excited than Nina seemed to be. Without the threat of aliens put to rest, Nina was still suspicious of the radio. After they said goodbye to Mr. Peebles, they stood near his stoop for twenty minutes trying to agree on what to do. Ada, of course, wanted to use her ham radio.

"There are so many interesting voices out there," said Ada. "I promise haven't heard one scary alien! *C'mon.* It'll be fun!"

"Yeah, I don't think so, Ada," said Nina.

"But what if I need you to really find the *other worlds*?" said Ada.

"Oh, Ada. I know you never believed in that," said Nina. "And I'm not sure I want to do that anymore. It's too weird and scary."

"But the world on the other side of my radio is the opposite of scary," said Ada. "There are different languages spoken and people of all ages and lifestyles doing cool and heroic things. Isn't that magical enough?"

"I guess," said Nina. "But there are also creeps playing mean pranks."

"I got rid of him!" said Ada. Nina didn't look convinced. "Okay. What would you rather do?"

"Play Apples to Apples?"

Ada hated that game.

"Uh. I guess," she said.

"Oh, never mind. Why don't you go talk to

your hams, and we can see each other in school on Monday?"

"Okay."

Ada had hoped she'd have a friend to share her hobby with. She would still enjoy it, but she wished she could enjoy it with Nina.

Chapter Seven

THE CREEP FACTOR

After Nina left, Ada tried to get ahold of the woman with the weather balloon, but she didn't have any luck. The girl in Marin wasn't around either. Then Milton tried to reach her.

KD8PKR. Are you there? Over.

. . .

KD8PKR? This is KD86E. Come in. Please? Over.

. . .

Ada? I know you're home. I saw you go inside. Over.

Leave me alone, Milton. Over and out.

Ada switched her radio off and tried to read. Then she played with George for a little while. She got him to go into Elliott's room to bring back her microscope. She didn't even really want to use it. She was just bored and avoiding Milton. Elliott didn't even seem to notice George. He was too busy going on an undersea adventure with Mr. Pickles. So she recorded a ghostly howling sound on George. It took a while to get the sound right, but then when she played it back, it sounded delightfully weird over his tiny speakers. She sent the robot back into Elliott's room with a command to play the sound thirty seconds after arrival. It worked perfectly.

"Woooooooooooooo!" sang George. "Wooooooooooo!"

"AAAAaaaaaahhhhhh!"

Ada peeked into Elliott's room from just outside her own. He was pressed against the wall, staring toward George, who was hidden under the corner of Elliott's bedspread.

"Dad! My room's haunted!" Ada ducked quickly back into her room.

Mr. Lace ran upstairs. "Elliott?! What's wrong, buddy?"

"There's a noise . . . a ghost noise," said Elliott.

Ada listened from just inside her doorway. She heard Elliott's comforter swish as Mr. Lace searched for the "ghost."

"It's just George. But you're right—that sound is spooky. Maybe there's something wrong with him," said Mr. Lace.

"He's haunted!" said Elliott.

"Ada?" Mr. Lace called.

Ada sat at her desk and tried to look like she was reading. Mr. Lace walked into her room, holding George. Ada tried to keep a straight face, but burst out laughing. She was so pleased that it had worked! Mr. Lace knew immediately that it was a prank, and he didn't think it was funny.

"Please leave your brother alone," he said. "Or there will be consequences."

"Yeah!" said Elliott, hiding behind his father. He was glad his sister was in trouble. And Ada was annoyed. If only she had been able to keep her cool. *It was just a joke,* she thought. Couldn't anyone take a joke? Then she remembered Milton. That's just what he had said about his prank. She had never really liked Milton—they were practically enemies from the moment she moved in. But somehow he was almost a different person over the radio. They had found something that they both ked, and they didn't really need to compete over vorked out better when they cooperated.

Ada switched on her radio. She tuned in to the frequency where she usually found Milton. She took a deep breath and pressed the bar on the mic.

KD86E? This is KD8PKR. Are you there? Over.

Well, well, well . . . if it isn't Ada. Over.

For once, she wasn't annoyed by Milton's voice.

How's it going, Milton?

A few days later, with a little help from Mr. Peebles, Milton and Ada arranged a time to talk to an astronaut on the International Space Station. Ada wrote down a list of questions. Milton said he was going to wing it. Ada wasn't sure how to feel about that. Would he be the prankster Milton? Or the helpful ham radio Milton? Time would tell.

Ada and Milton had been having fun "hamming it up," as her father liked to say, but she still missed Nina. Even though they still walked to and from school together, still sat together at lunch, and still chatted online, Ada had a big portion of her life that she wasn't sharing with her best friend. So she invited Nina over to talk to NASA. It was on Thursday night after dinner, so they had to get extra special permission for Nina to come over. Milton and Mr. Peebles would be on their own radios at home.

Nina still didn't trust the radio. She sat on the bed looking through a magazine while Ada scanned through different frequencies. The time crawled by.

"Do you really trust Milton not to mess it up?" said Nina. "Or joke around with make-believe aliens? Or pull a prank or make fun of me?"

"I don't know, Nina," said Ada. "He's Milton. [illegible]lways have to be on the lookout with him a [illegible]"

“Or a lotta bit,” said Nina.

Ada paused on a ham frequency where two kids were singing “Three Little Birds” to their dad. George switched on and started playing his own version.

“Ha!” Nina laughed. “George’s favorite!”

“Mine too!” said Ada. “I think it’s a good sign. Don’t you?”

“Maybe,” said Nina.

The kids said good night, and the radio was silent.

"But, you know, if aliens come on—pretend or real—I might bolt right out that door, right? I mean, I might not be able to stop myself."

"I'm pretty sure there won't be any aliens this time," said Ada. "But if there are, we'll get through it together."

Chapter Eight

Making Contact

It took some time. They had to wait until the space station was directly overhead in order to connect, but when they finally did, it was surprising how close the astronaut sounded. She might have been in the next city, rather than 250 miles above the Earth. The astronaut they spoke to was named Sandy. She had been on the space station for three months. Mr. Peebles let Ada, Nina, and Milton do most of the talking.

Sandy, this is Milton. How do you get oxygen to the space station? Over.

Well, Milton, we can actually make it up here! Believe it or not, we just take water—which you probably know has two hydrogen atoms and one oxygen atom—and we separate it to get the oxygen out. Over.

Hi, Sandy. It's Ada. Do you use electrolysis? Over.

Yes, that's exactly right, Ada. We pass electric current through the water, and that separates the oxygen from the hydrogen. Over.

Sandy, this is Milton again. How long are you up there for? Over.

I'm lucky! I have another three months. The missions vary from a couple of weeks to six months, and I got one that was on the longer side. Over.

There was a long pause as Ada tried to pull Nina toward the mic. Nina was being shy. Ada was afraid that Milton would hog all the time if they let him, so she jumped in.

Sandy? It's Ada again. What are you doing up there right now? Over.

We're collecting all kinds of data about the Earth—temperature, climate patterns, weather, pollution. It helps us get a sense of the Earth's health.

Finally, Nina jumped in.

Sandy, this is Nina. Can you see San Francisco from up there? Over.

I can! Cities are beautiful from space—like clusters of Christmas lights. Nature can be pretty amazing too. Believe it or not, I can also see things like the Great Barrier Reef sometimes. You can see pictures of what we see from the space station on our website. Over.

Nina again. Do you ever get lonely? Over.

A little bit. I have my colleagues here, and I get along with all of them pretty well. We all feel excited about what we're doing. And I get to talk to people like you and my family and friends. But it's a strange feeling seeing your home planet from above. It's like looking at the moon or Mars from Earth, but instead it's the place you were born, so you feel a little more attached to it. Like it's your responsibility. And you

want to protect it. So I do miss my home. I miss all the paths I used to walk on near Boulder when I lived there. I miss the smell of the air and how the creek water feels on my feet. But up here I have the opportunity to study what makes those things possible and how to keep them from going away. That was a long answer, I guess. Anyway, I'm glad I get to play a little part in helping to monitor the Earth's health. Over.

Sandy, it's Ada. How do you monitor the climate patterns? Over.

That's a fun question! We actually released a swarm of little satellites last week. . . .

Nina's eyes grew. For a second Ada was afraid she might flee the room.

Each little satellite has a different part to play. They are mostly monitoring how much radiation is coming into the Earth's atmosphere versus how much is leaving. Over.

Sandy, it's Arnold Peebles. Thank you for talking to us. Good luck up there. We're rooting for you. Over and out.

Nina looked at Ada. "The swarm," said Nina. "It was a swarm of little satellites. I must have heard them talking right when they released them."

"Right," said Ada. "We must have been lined up just right that night. So the space station must have been directly above us! No trees to block the signal."

"And I woke up at just the right moment,"

said Nina. "And they were sent to help us. Not invade us."

"So it is a little magic," said Ada. Nina smiled.

Ada opened her computer to look at the space station pictures. She thought it would be fun to see the Earth as Sandy described it.

"Wow, there's Mount Vesuvius!" said Ada.

"The cities are pretty. Look at the Nile! It's like a glowing snake," said Nina.

"Yeah!" said Ada. She liked the way Nina

described things. "Ooo! Look! This city looks just like a campfire."

"Hey, there's San Francisco!"

"Which picture do you think is the best?" asked Ada.

"I like the Himalayas. And the Sahara Desert. And Scandinavia at night. How can you pick a favorite?" asked Nina. "It's all beautiful."

"It sure is," said Ada.

After Mr. Lace had taken Nina home and Ada was about to turn off the radio and get into bed, Milton called one more time.

Ada, are you still up? Over.

Ada was so tired she thought about ignoring him, but she was kind of curious about what he had to say.

Ada, Ada, Ada. Are you there? Over.

Yeah, Milton. I'm here. What's up? Over.

I made a gimbal for my little camera. You know, so it doesn't shake so much when it's up on the kite. I'm thinking about flying it in the park . . . maybe tomorrow. You wanna join me? Over.

Ada didn't answer right away.

Ada? Are you still there? Over.

Sure, Milton. I'll join you. See you tomorrow. Over and out.

Behind the Science

SMART HOUSE

Ada has programmed her robot, George, to control different technologies in her room. This is actually pretty easy to do, as long as you have the right equipment! For example, I use a Google Home device (my version of George) to control all the lights in my apartment. When I get home, I can just say "Okay, Google, turn on the kitchen lights" or "Okay, Google, dim lights to 50 percent," and the Google Home will connect to the lights and do it. I had to buy special light bulbs that connect to the Internet in order to do this. Basically my Google Home talks to the light bulbs over Wi-Fi and changes what I tell it to change. Ada could do the same thing with different technologies, like a specialized sprinkler system. Building your own smart room is a fun way to use technology to make your life a bit easier, as long as it's working properly!

Ham Radio

Hundreds of thousands of people around the world use ham radios to communicate with each other. It's a fun hobby and a useful way to contact others. You can be in the middle of nowhere, with no cell phone service, and communicate with another hobbyist with a ham radio. To speak with someone over a ham radio, you should announce yourself using your call sign, which you get after you pass a specific test and earn your ham radio license. I received my license while I was studying in school at MIT. Did you notice Ada's call sign, KD8PKR? That's actually my call sign! You can get one yourself, too. If you're interested, check out the American Radio Relay League (arrl.org) for more information.

Radio Repeater

Some radio signals can be blocked by tall trees, buildings, or even hilltops. Because of this, radio repeaters are frequently used in the ham radio community and are placed on some of the highest locations around town. A repeater will take a signal and then retransmit it to the other side of a tall tree, building, hilltop, or wherever the repeater was placed. It's kind of like if you wanted to shine a laser at your friend, but a long wall was in between you and her. How would you get the laser beam to reach her? Well, imagine if there was a mirror perfectly placed on top of the wall, so that you could look at the mirror and see your friend on the other side. If you pointed your laser at that mirror, the laser beam would bounce off it and hit your friend!

Like a mirror, a repeater will receive a radio signal and make sure it gets to the other side of a high barrier. Thanks to Ada's repeater, she can finally send and receive signals beyond Juniper Garden!

Contacting Aliens

Throughout the book, Nina is afraid that aliens from another world are trying to contact them. Interestingly, she's not entirely wrong about that possibility. Today we have many different radio telescopes around the world (they look like huge bowls) that are listening for alien radio transmissions. Scientists believe that if there is other intelligent life out there, it probably uses technology. And because a lot of our most advanced technologies emit radio waves, listening for radio waves that may be coming from other planets in our universe may just be the best way to find ET!

Radio Waves

Radio waves are just one type of wave in the electromagnetic spectrum. Microwaves, X-rays, and even the light you can see with your own eyes are different types of waves in the electromagnetic spectrum. All these waves have different wavelengths, some larger than others. Radio waves have the largest wavelengths of them all. X-rays and gamma rays have the shortest wavelengths and can actually be pretty dangerous if you're exposed to them but not properly protected! The light you see with your eye is somewhere in the middle. Radio waves are really useful to humans—we use them all the time! Radio waves are used to connect your iPad to the Internet, and to transmit TV shows, cell phone calls, and, of course, radio stations. It would certainly be hard for any town to function if we didn't have radio waves!

Earth-Observing Satellites

Our planet's climate is changing, and one of the ways we know that is because of satellites that orbit our planet, sending images and measurements back to scientists here on Earth. For example, NASA has an "Earth Observing System" that includes more than fifteen satellites that study the atmosphere, ice sheets, oceans, and other parts of the environment. Using information from these satellites, scientists have figured out that the Earth *is* warming up, and the climate is changing quickly due to human activities like burning fossil fuels. As we figure out how to make cleaner technologies and how to stop the Earth from warming, swarms of satellites will keep a watchful eye on the Earth and how we're changing it.

Speaking to an Astronaut

Mr. Peebles helps Ada, Nina, and Milton contact an astronaut in space using a ham radio. The coolest part about this is that it is actually something that you can do in real life—I've done it! I spoke to an astronaut on the International Space Station on a ham radio with a bunch of other students through a program called ARISS. The type of ham radio that Ada uses, a 2-meter radio, emits the right type of radio wave that can zip though Earth's atmosphere and go into space. (Not all electromagnetic waves can do that—some actually bounce back!)

Remember in the beginning of the story, when Nina heard the radio transmit "Release the swarm" even though the ham radio wasn't picking up any other signal at the time? This was because the trees in Juniper Garden were blocking Ada's signal from leaving the neighborhood, but the trees weren't blocking her ham radio from receiving signals from overhead—from space! The International Space Station must have been directly above them at the time—and they were just lucky enough to hear its transmission.

ACKNOWLEDGMENTS

As a kid who grew up in West Virginia, I found myself on a lot of back roads late at night with my family. We'd be thirty minutes outside the city, away from all the light pollution, driving back home from a family member's house. I'd lean my head against the window and look up at the night sky, following the stars all the way home. This is when I would daydream about aliens.

Fantasizing about life on different planets sparked my imagination like nothing else. It made the universe feel exciting, wild, and new—just waiting to be explored. That spark led to a career in the space industry that I will forever be grateful for, so I'm thankful to the beautiful state of West Virginia for giving me a dark night sky to see the universe. Every kid should have a safe, dark place to daydream about the universe.

As always, thank you to my incredible Ada Lace team for keeping the adventures going: Liz Kossnar at Simon & Schuster Books for Young Readers, Kyell Thomas and Jennifer Keene at Octagon, Tamson Weston, and Renée Kurilla—you're all so talented, and Ada and I are lucky to have you.